About the Author

LOUISE ERDRICH is the author of sixteen novels as well as volumes of poetry, children's books, short stories, and a memoir of early motherhood. Her novel *LaRose* won the National Book Critics Circle Award in fiction, while *The Round House* received the National Book Award for fiction. *The Plague of Doves* was a finalist for the Pulitzer Prize. Erdrich has received the Library of Congress Prize in American Fiction and the prestigious PEN/Saul Bellow Award for Achievement in American Fiction. She is a Turtle Mountain Chippewa and lives in Minnesota with her daughters. She is the owner of Birchbark Books, a small independent bookstore.

Original Fire

Original Fire

Selected and New Poems

Louise Erdrich

HARPER PERENNIAL

NEW YORK • LONDON • TORONTO • SYDNEY • NEW DELHI • AUCKLAND

HARPER ● PERENNIAL

The author would like to thank and acknowledge the editors of *Georgia Review*, in which "Time" originally appeared in slightly different form.

A hardcover edition of this book was published in 2003 by HarperCollins Publishers.

HarperCollins books may be purchased for educational, business, or sales pro-motional use. For information, please email the Special Markets Department at SPsales@harpercollins.com.

First Perennial edition published 2004; reissued in 2018.

Designed by Joseph Rutt

Library of Congress Cataloging-in-Publication Data is available.

ISBN 978-0-06-093534-4 (pbk.)

18 19 20 21 22 ❖/LSC 10 9 8 7 6 5 4 3 2 1

To Pallas

Contents

Jacklight

The Potchikoo Stories

The Butcher's Wife

The Seven Sleepers

Original Fire

Jacklight

Jacklight

The same Chippewa word is used both for flirting and hunting game,
while another Chippewa word connotes both using force in intercourse
and also killing a bear with one's bare hands.

—R. W. Dunning, *Social and*
Economic Change Among the
Northern Ojibwa (1959)

We have come to the edge of the woods,
out of brown grass where we slept, unseen,
out of knotted twigs, out of leaves creaked shut,
out of hiding.

At first the light wavered, glancing over us.
Then it clenched to a fist of light that pointed,
searched out, divided us.
Each took the beams like direct blows the heart answers.
Each of us moved forward alone.

We have come to the edge of the woods,
drawn out of ourselves by this night sun,
this battery of polarized acids,
that outshines the moon.

We smell them behind it
but they are faceless, invisible.
We smell the raw steel of their gun barrels,
mink oil on leather, their tongues of sour barley.
We smell their mothers buried chin-deep in wet dirt.
We smell their fathers with scoured knuckles,
teeth cracked from hot marrow.
We smell their sisters of crushed dogwood, bruised apples,
of fractured cups and concussions of burnt hooks.

We smell their breath steaming lightly behind the jacklight.
We smell the itch underneath the caked guts on their clothes.
We smell their minds like silver hammers
cocked back, held in readiness
for the first of us to step into the open.

We have come to the edge of the woods,
out of brown grass where we slept, unseen,
out of leaves creaked shut, out of hiding.
We have come here too long.

It is their turn now,
their turn to follow us. Listen,
they put down their equipment.
It is useless in the tall brush.

And now they take the first steps, now knowing
how deep the woods are and lightless.
How deep the woods are.

The Woods

At one time your touches were clothing enough.
Within these trees now I am different.
Now I wear the woods.

I lower a headdress of bent sticks and secure it.
I strap to myself a breastplate of clawed, roped bark.
I fit the broad leaves of sugar maples
to my hands, like mittens of blood.

Now when I say *come*,
and you enter the woods,
hunting some creature like the woman I was,
I surround you.

Light bleeds from the clearing. Roots rise.
Fluted molds burn blue in the falling light,
and you also know
the loneliness that you taught me with your body.

When you lie down in the grave of a slashed tree,
I cover you, as I always did.
Only this time you do not leave.

The Strange People

*The antelope are strange people ... they are beautiful to look at, and yet
they are tricky. We do not trust them. They appear and disappear; they are
like shadows on the plains. Because of their great beauty, young men
sometimes follow the antelope and are lost forever. Even if those foolish
ones find themselves and return, they are never again right in their heads.*

　　　　　　　　　　　　　　——Pretty Shield,
　　　　　　　　　　　　　　　　Medicine Woman of the Crows
　　　　　　　　　　　　　　　　transcribed and edited by
　　　　　　　　　　　　　　　　Frank Linderman (1932)

All night I am the doe, breathing
his name in a frozen field,
the small mist of the word
drifting always before me.

And again he has heard it
and I have gone burning
to meet him, the jacklight
fills my eyes with blue fire;
the heart in my chest
explodes like a hot stone.

Then slung like a sack
in the back of his pickup,
I wipe the death scum
from my mouth, sit up laughing
and shriek in my speeding grave.

Safely shut in the garage,
when he sharpens his knife
and thinks to have me, like that,
I come toward him,
a lean gray witch
through the bullets that enter and dissolve.

I sit in his house
drinking coffee till dawn
and leave as frost reddens on hubcaps,
crawling back into my shadowy body.
All day, asleep in clean grasses,
I dream of the one who could really wound me.
Not with weapons, not with a kiss, not with a look.
Not even with his goodness.

If a man was never to lie to me. *Never lie me.*
I swear I would never leave him.

Captivity

He (my captor) gave me a bisquit, which I put in my pocket, and not daring to eat it, buried it under a log, fearing he had put something in it to make me love him.

> —From the narrative of the
> captivity of Mrs. Mary
> Rowlandson, who was taken
> prisoner by the Wampanoag
> when Lancaster, Massachusetts,
> was destroyed, in the year 1676

The stream was swift, and so cold
I thought I would be sliced in two.
But he dragged me from the flood
by the ends of my hair.
I had grown to recognize his face.
I could distinguish it from the others.
There were times I feared I understood
his language, which was not human,
and I knelt to pray for strength.

We were pursued by God's agents
or pitch devils, I did not know.
Only that we must march.
Their guns were loaded with swan shot.

I could not suckle and my child's wail
put them in danger.
He had a woman
with teeth black and glittering.
She fed the child milk of acorns.
The forest closed, the light deepened.

I told myself that I would starve
before I took food from his hands
but I did not starve.
One night
he killed a deer with a young one in her
and gave me to eat of the fawn.
It was so tender,
the bones like the stems of flowers,
that I followed where he took me.
The night was thick. He cut the cord
that bound me to the tree.

After that the birds mocked.
Shadows gaped and roared
and the trees flung down
their sharpened lashes.
He did not notice God's wrath.
God blasted fire from half-buried stumps.
I hid my face in my dress, fearing He would burn us all
but this, too, passed.

Rescued, I see no truth in things.
My husband drives a thick wedge
through the earth, still it shuts
to him year after year.
My child is fed of the first wheat.
I lay myself to sleep
on a Holland-laced pillowbeer.
I lay to sleep.
And in the dark I see myself
as I was outside their circle.

They knelt on deerskins, some with sticks,
and he led his company in the noise
until I could no longer bear
the thought of how I was.
I stripped a branch
and struck the earth,
in time, begging it to open
to admit me
as he was
and feed me honey from the rock.

Owls

The barred owls scream in the black pines,
searching for mates. Each night
the noise wakes me, a death
rattle, everything in sex that wounds.
There is nothing in the sound but raw need
of one feathered body for another.
Yet, even when they find each other,
there is no peace.

In Ojibwe, the owl is Kokoko, and not
even the smallest child loves the gentle sound
of the word. Because the hairball
of bones and vole teeth can be hidden
under snow, to kill the man who walks over it.
Because the owl looks behind itself to see you coming,
the vane of the feather does not disturb
air, and the barb is ominously soft.

Have you ever seen, at dusk,
an owl take flight from the throat of a dead tree?
Mist, troubled spirit.
You will notice only after
its great silver body has turned to bark.
The flight was soundless.

That is how we make love,
when there are people in the halls around us,
clashing dishes, filling their mouths
with air, with debris, pulling
switches and filters as the whole machinery
of life goes on, eliminating and eliminating
until there are just the two bodies
fiercely attached, the feathers
floating down and cleaving to their shapes.

I Was Sleeping Where the Black Oaks Move

We watched from the house
as the river grew, helpless
and terrible in its unfamiliar body.
Wrestling everything into it,
the water wrapped around trees
until their life-hold was broken.
They went down, one by one,
and the river dragged off their covering.

Nests of the herons, roots washed to bones,
snags of soaked bark on the shoreline:
a whole forest pulled through the teeth
of the spillway. Trees surfacing
singly, where the river poured off
into arteries for fields below the reservation.

When at last it was over, the long removal,
they had all become the same dry wood.
We walked among them, the branches
whitening in the raw sun.
Above us drifted herons,
alone, hoarse-voiced, broken,
settling their beaks among the hollows.

Grandpa said, *These are the ghosts of the tree people*
moving among us, unable to take their rest.

Sometimes now, we dream our way back to the heron dance.
Their long wings are bending the air
into circles through which they fall.
They rise again in shifting wheels.
How long must we live in the broken figures
their necks make, narrowing the sky.

Family Reunion

Ray's third new car in half as many years.
Full cooler in the trunk, Ray sogging the beer
as I solemnly chauffeur us through the bush
and up the backroads, hardly cowpaths and hub-deep in mud.
All day the sky lowers, clears, lowers again.
Somewhere in the bush near Saint John
there are uncles, a family, one mysterious brother
who stayed on the land when Ray left for the cities.
One week Ray is crocked. We've been through this before.
Even, as a little girl, hands in my dress,
Ah punka, you's my Debby, come and ki me.

Then the road ends in a yard full of dogs.
Them's Indian dogs, Ray says, lookit how they know me.
And they do seem to know him, like I do. His odor—
rank beef of fierce turtle pulled dripping from Metagoshe,
and the inflammable mansmell: hair tonic, ashes, alcohol.
Ray dances an old woman up in his arms.
Fiddles reel in the phonograph and I sink apart
in a corner, start knocking the Blue Ribbons down.
Four generations of people live here.
No one remembers Raymond Twobears.

So what. The walls shiver, the old house caulked with mud
sails back into the middle of Metagoshe.
A three-foot-long snapper is hooked on a fishline,
so mean that we do not dare wrestle him in
but tow him to shore, heavy as an old engine.
Then somehow Ray pries the beak open and shoves
down a cherry bomb. Lights the string tongue.

Headless and clenched in its armor, the snapper
is lugged home in the trunk for tomorrow's soup.
Ray rolls it beneath a bush in the backyard and goes in
to sleep his own head off. Tomorrow I find
that the animal has dragged itself off.
I follow torn tracks up a slight hill and over
into a small stream that deepens and widens into a marsh.

Ray finds his way back through the room into his arms.
When the phonograph stops, he slumps hard in his hands
and the boys and their old man fold him into the car
where he curls around his bad heart, hearing how it knocks
and rattles at the bars of his ribs to break out.

Somehow we find our way back. Uncle Ray
sings an old song to the body that pulls him
toward home. The gray fins that his hands have become
screw their bones in the dashboard. His face
has the odd, calm patience of a child who has always

let bad wounds alone, or a creature that has lived for a long time underwater. And the angels come lowering their slings and litters.

Indian Boarding School: The Runaways

Home's the place we head for in our sleep.
Boxcars stumbling north in dreams
don't wait for us. We catch them on the run.
The rails, old lacerations that we love,
shoot parallel across the face and break
just under Turtle Mountains. Riding scars
you can't get lost. Home is the place they cross.

The lame guard strikes a match and makes the dark
less tolerant. We watch through cracks in boards
as the land starts rolling, rolling till it hurts
to be here, cold in regulation clothes.
We know the sheriff's waiting at midrun
to take us back. His car is dumb and warm.
The highway doesn't rock, it only hums
like a wing of long insults. The worn-down welts
of ancient punishments lead back and forth.

All runaways wear dresses, long green ones,
the color you would think shame was. We scrub
the sidewalks down because it's shameful work.
Our brushes cut the stone in watered arcs
and in the soak frail outlines shiver clear

a moment, things us kids pressed on the dark
face before it hardened, pale, remembering
delicate old injuries, the spines of names and leaves.

Dear John Wayne

August and the drive-in picture is packed.
We lounge on the hood of the Pontiac
surrounded by the slow-burning spirals they sell
at the window, to vanquish the hordes of mosquitoes.
Nothing works. They break through the smoke screen for blood.

Always the lookout spots the Indians first,
spread north to south, barring progress.
The Sioux or some other Plains bunch
in spectacular columns, ICBM missiles,
feathers bristling in the meaningful sunset.

The drum breaks. There will be no parlance.
Only the arrows whining, a death-cloud of nerves
swarming down on the settlers
who die beautifully, tumbling like dust weeds
into the history that brought us all here
together: this wide screen beneath the sign of the bear.

The sky fills, acres of blue squint and eye
that the crowd cheers. His face moves over us,
a thick cloud of vengeance, pitted
like the land that was once flesh. Each rut,

each scar makes a promise: It is
not over, this fight, not as long as you resist.

Everything we see belongs to us.

A few laughing Indians fall over the hood
slipping in the hot spilled butter.
The eye sees a lot, John, but the heart is so blind.
Death makes us owners of nothing.
He smiles, a horizon of teeth
the credits reel over, and then the white fields

again blowing in the true-to-life dark.
The dark films over everything.
We get into the car
scratching our mosquito bites, speechless and small
as people are when the movie is done.
We are back in our skins.

How can we help but keep hearing his voice,
the flip side of the sound track, still playing:
Come on, boys, we got them
where we want them, drunk, running.
They'll give us what we want, what we need.
Even his disease was the idea of taking everything.
Those cells, burning, doubling, splitting out of their skins.

Manitoulin Ghost

Once there was a girl who died in a fire in this house, here on Bidwell
road. Now she keeps coming back, trying to hitch a ride out of here. Watch
out for her at night and do not stop.

         —Mary Lou Fox

Each night she waits by the road
in a thin, white dress
embroidered with fire.

It has been twenty years
since her house surged and burst in the dark trees.
Still, nobody goes there.

The heat charred the branches
of the apple trees,
but nothing can kill that wood.

She will climb into your car
but not say where she is going
and you shouldn't ask.

Nor should you try to comb the blackened nest of hair
or press the agates of tears
back into her eyes.

First the orchard bowed low and complained
of the unpicked fruit,
then the branches cracked apart and fell.

The windfalls sweetened to wine
beneath the ruined arms and snow.
Each spring now, in the grass, buds form on the tattered wood.

The child, the child, why is she so persistent
in her need? Is it so terrible
to be alone when the cold white blossoms
come to life and burn?

Three Sisters

One sister wore the eyes of an old man
around her neck.
Scratched porcelain
washed down
with the hot lye of his breath.

One sister rode love
like a ship in light wind.
The sails of her body
unfurled at a touch.
No man could deny her
safe passage, safe harbor.

The youngest was shut like a bell.
The white thorns of silence
pricked in each bush
where she walked,
and the grass stopped growing where she stood.

One year the three sisters came out of their rooms,
swaying like the hot roses
that papered their walls.
They walked, full grown, into the heart of our town.

Young men broke their eyes
against their eyes of stone,
and singed their shy tongues
on the stunned flames of their mouths.

It was in late August in the long year of drought.
The pool halls were winnowed
and three men drew lots
to marry the sisters, all six in a great house.

On the night of the wedding
the wind rose on a glass stem.
The trees bowed. The clouds knocked.
We tethered our dogs.

Some swore they saw a hoop
of lightning dance down in their yard.
We felt the weight toward dawn
of lead sinkers in our bones,
walked out, and caught the first, fast drops on our tongues.

The Lefavor Girls

All autumn, black plums
split and dropped from the boughs.
We gathered the sweetness
and sealed it in jars,
loading the cupboards and cellar.

At night we went under the bedclothes, laden
beyond what the arms were meant to carry alone,
and we dreamed that with our shirts off
in the quarry, the cool water
came under to bear us away.

That season our sleep grew around us
as if from the walls
a dense snow fell and formed
other bodies, and the voices
of men who melted into us,
and children who drifted, lost, looking for home.

After the long rains, the land gone bare,
we walked out again to the windbreaks.
White crown of the plum trees
were filling the purple throats of the iris.

We lay in the grass,
the bees drinking in tongues,
and already the brittle hum of the locust
in the red wheat, growing.

Again, the year come full circle, the men
came knocking in the fields,
headfuls of blackened seeds,
and the husking, scorched mountains of sunflowers.

We went closed, still golden, among the harvesters.
Shifting the load from arm to arm,
they drove us into town.
We shook out our dresses and hair, oh then

There was abundance come down
in the face of the coming year.
We held ourselves into
the wind, our bodies
broke open, and the snow began falling.

It fell until the world was filled up, and filled again,
until it rose past all the limits we could have known.

Walking in the Breakdown Lane

Wind has stripped
the young plum trees
to a thin howl.
They are planted in squares
to keep the loose dirt from wandering.
Everything around me is crying to be gone.
The fields, the crops humming to be cut and done with.

Walking in the breakdown lane, margin of gravel,
between the cut swaths and the road to Fargo,
I want to stop, to lie down
in standing wheat or standing water.

Behind me thunder mounts as trucks of cattle
roar over, faces pressed to slats for air.
They go on, they go on without me.
They pound, pound and bawl,
until the road closes over them farther on.

The Red Sleep of Beasts

On space of about an acre I counted two hundred and twenty of these animals; the banks of the river were covered thus with these animals as far as the eye could reach and in all directions. One may judge now, if it is possible, the richness of these prairies.

—From a letter by Father Belcourt,
a priest who accompanied the
Turtle Mountain Michif on one
of their last buffalo hunts in
the 1840s, in *North Dakota
Historical Collections*, volume 5

We heard them when they left the hills,
Low hills where they used to winter and bear their young.
Blue hills of oak and birch that broke the wind.
They swung their heavy muzzles, wet with steam,
And broke their beards of breath to breathe.

We used to hunt them in our red-wheeled carts.
Frenchmen gone *sauvage*, how the women burned
In scarlet sashes, black wool skirts.
For miles you heard the ungreased wood
Groan as the load turned.

Thunder was the last good hunt.
Great bales of skins and meat in iron cauldrons
Boiling through the night. We made our feast
All night, but still we could not rest.

We lived headlong, taking what we could
But left no scraps behind, not like the other
Hide hunters, hidden on a rise,
Their long-eyes brought herds one by one
To earth. They took but tongue, and you could walk
For miles across the strange hulks.

We wintered in the hills. Low huts of log
And trampled dirt, the spaces tamped with mud.
At night we touched each other in our dreams
Hearing, on the wind, their slow hooves stumbling

South, we said at first, the old ones knew
They would not come again to the low hills.
We heard them traveling, heard the frozen birches
Break before their long retreat
Into the red sleep.

The Potchikoo Stories

The Birth of Potchikoo

You don't have to believe this, I'm not asking you to. But Potchikoo claims that his father is the sun in heaven that shines down on us all.

There was a very pretty Chippewa girl working in a field once. She was digging potatoes for a farmer someplace around Pembina when suddenly the wind blew her dress up around her face and wrapped her apron so tightly around her arms that she couldn't move. She lay helplessly in the dust with her potato sack, this poor girl, and as she lay there she felt the sun shining down very steadily upon her.

Then she felt something else. You know what. I don't have to say it. She cried out for her mother.

This girl's mother came running and untangled her daughter's clothes. When she freed the girl, she saw that there were tears in her daughter's eyes. Bit by bit, the mother coaxed out the story. After the girl told what had happened to her, the mother just shook her head sadly.

"I don't know what we can expect now," she said.

Well nine months passed and he was born looking just like a potato with tough warty skin and a puckered round shape. All the ladies came to visit the girl and left saying things behind their hands.

"That's what she gets for playing loose in the potato fields," they said.

But the girl didn't care what they said after a while because she used to go and stand alone in a secret clearing in the woods and let the sun shine steadily upon her. Sometimes she took her little potato boy. She noticed when the sun shone on him he grew and became a little more human-looking.

One day the girl fell asleep in the sun with her potato boy next to her. The sun beat down so hard on him that he had an enormous spurt of growth. When the girl woke up, her son was fully grown. He said good-bye to his mother then, and went out to see what was going on in the world.

Potchikoo Marries

After he had several adventures, the potato boy took the name Potchikoo and decided to try married life.

I'll just see what it's like for a while, he thought, and then I'll start wandering again.

How very inexperienced he was!

He took the train to Minneapolis to find a wife and as soon as he got off he saw her. She was a beautiful Indian girl standing at the door to a little shop where they sold cigarettes and pipe tobacco. How proud she looked! How peaceful. She was so lovely that she made Potchikoo shy. He could hardly look at her.

Potchikoo walked into the store and bought some cigarettes. He lit one up and stuck it between the beautiful woman's lips. Then he stood next to her, still too shy to look at her, until he smelled smoke. He saw that she had somehow caught fire.

"Oh, I'll save you!" cried Potchikoo.

He grabbed his lady love and ran with her to the lake, which was, handily, across the street. He threw her in. At first he was afraid she would drown but soon she floated to the surface and kept floating away from Potchikoo. This made him angry.

"Trying to run away already!" he shouted.

He leaped in to catch her. But he had forgotten that he couldn't swim. So Potchikoo had to hang on to his wooden sweetheart while she drifted slowly all the way across the lake. When they got to the other side of the lake, across from Minneapolis, they were in wilderness. As soon as the wooden girl touched the shore she became alive and jumped up and dragged Potchikoo out of the water.

"I'll teach you to shove a cigarette between my lips like that," she said, beating him with her fists, which were still hard as wood. "Now that you're my husband you'll do things my way!"

That was how Potchikoo met and married Josette. He was married to her all his life. After she made it clear what she expected of her husband, Josette made a little toboggan of cut saplings and tied him upon it. Then she decided she never wanted to see Minneapolis again. She wanted to live in the hills. That is why she dragged Potchikoo all the way back across Minnesota to the Turtle Mountains, where they spent all the years of their wedded bliss.

How Potchikoo Got Old

As a young man, Potchikoo sometimes embarrassed his wife by breaking wind during Holy Mass. It was for this reason that Josette whittled him a little plug out of ash wood and told him to put it in that place before he entered Saint Ann's church.

Potchikoo did as she asked, and even said a certain charm over the plug so that it would not be forced out, no matter what. Then the two of them entered the church to say their prayers.

That Sunday, Father Belcourt was giving a special sermon on the ascension of the Lord Christ to heaven. It happened in the twinkling of an eye, he said, with no warning, because Christ was more pure than air. How surprised everyone was to see, as Father Belcourt said this, the evil scoundrel Potchikoo rising from his pew!

His hands were folded, and his closed eyes and meek face wore a look of utter piety. He didn't even seem to realize he was rising, he prayed so hard.

Up and up he floated, still in the kneeling position, until he reached the dark blue vault of the church. He seemed to inflate, too, until he looked larger than life to the people. They were on the verge of believing it a miracle when all of a sudden it happened. Bang! Even with the charm the little ash-wood plug could not contain the wind of Potchikoo. Out it popped, and Potchikoo went buzzing and sputtering around the church the way balloons do when children let go of the ends.

Holy Mass was canceled for a week so the church could be aired out, but to this day a faint scent still lingers, and Potchikoo, sadly enough, was shriveled by his sudden collapse and flight through the air. For when Josette picked him up to bring home, she found that he was now wrinkled and dry like an old man.

The Death of Potchikoo

Once there were three stones sitting in a patch of soft slough mud. Each of these stones had the smooth round shape of a woman's breast, but no one had ever noticed this—that is, not until Old Man Potchikoo walked through the woods. He was the type who always noticed this kind of thing. As soon as he saw the three stones, Potchikoo sat down on a small bank of grass to enjoy what he saw.

He was not really much of a connoisseur, the old man. He just knew what he liked when he saw it. The three stones were light brown in color, delicately veined, and so smooth that they almost looked slippery. Old Man Potchikoo began to wonder if they really were slippery, and then he thought of touching them.

They were in the middle of the soft slough mud, so the old man took his boots and socks off. Then he thought of his wife Josette and what she would say if he came home with mud on his clothes. He took off his shirt and pants. He never wore undershorts. Wading toward those stones, he was as naked as them.

He had to kneel in the mud to touch the stones, and when he did this he sank to his thighs. But oh, when he touched the stones, he found that they were bigger than they looked from the shore and so shiny, so slippery. His hands polished them, and polished them some more, and before he knew it, that Potchikoo was making love to the slough.

Years passed by. The Potchikoos got older and more frail. One day Josette went into town, and as he always did as soon as she was out of sight, Potchikoo sat down on his front steps to do nothing.

As he sat there, he saw three women walk very slowly out of the woods. They walked across the field and then walked slowly toward him. As they drew near, Potchikoo saw that they were just his kind of women. They were large, their hair was black and very long, and because they wore low-cut blouses, he could see that their breasts were beautiful—light brown, delicately veined, and so smooth they looked slippery.

"We are your daughters," they said, standing before him. "We are from the slough."

A faint memory stirred in Potchikoo as he looked at their breasts, and he smiled.

"Oh my daughters," he said to them. "Yes I remember you. Come sit on your daddy's lap and get acquainted."

The daughters moved slowly toward Potchikoo. As he saw their skin up close, he marveled at how fine it was, smooth as polished stone. The first daughter sank upon his knee and clasped her arms around him. She was so heavy that the old man couldn't move. Then the others sank upon him, blocking away the sun with their massive bodies. The old man's head began to swim and yellow stars turned in his skull. He hardly knew it when all three daughters laid their heads dreamily against his chest. They were cold, and so heavy that his ribs snapped apart like little dry twigs.

Potchikoo's Life After Death

How They Don't Let Potchikoo into Heaven

After Old Man Potchikoo died, the people had a funeral for his poor, crushed body, and everyone felt sorry for the things they had said while he was alive. Josette went home and set some bread by the door for him to take on his journey to the next world. Then she began to can a bucket of plums she'd bought cheap, because they were overripe.

As she canned, she thought how it was. Now she'd have to give away these sweet plums since they had been her husband's favorites. She didn't like plums. Her tastes ran sour. Everything about her did. As she worked, she cried vinegar tears into the jars before she sealed them. People would later remark on her ingenuity. No one else on the reservation pickled plums.

Now, as night fell, Potchikoo got out of his body, and climbed up through the dirt. He took the frybread Josette had left in a towel, his provisions. He looked in the window, saw she was sleeping alone, and he was satisfied. Of course, since he never could hold himself back, he immediately ate the bread as he walked the long road, a mistake. Two days later, he was terribly hungry, and there was no end in sight. He came to the huge luscious berry he knew he shouldn't eat if he wanted to enter the heaven all the priests and nuns described. He took a little bite, and told himself he'd not touch the rest. But it tasted so good tears came to his eyes. It took a minute, hardly that, for him to stuff the whole berry by handfuls into his mouth.

He didn't know what would happen now, but the road was still there. He kept walking, but he'd become so fat from his greed that when he came to the log bridge, a test for good souls, he couldn't balance to cross it, fell in repeatedly, and went on cold and shivering. But he was dry again, and warmer, by the time he reached the pearly gates.

Saint Peter was standing there, dressed in a long, brown robe, just as the nuns and priests had always said he would be. He examined Potchikoo back and front for berry stains, but they had luckily washed away when Potchikoo fell off the bridge.

"What's your name?" Saint Peter asked.

Potchikoo told him, and then Saint Peter pulled a huge book out from under his robe. As the saint's finger traveled down the lists, Potchikoo became frightened to think how many awful deeds would be recorded after his name. But as it happened, there was only one word there. The word *Indian*.

"Ah," Saint Peter said. "You'll have to keep walking."

Where Potchikoo Goes Next

So he kept on. As he walked, the road, which had been nicely paved and lit when it got near heaven, narrowed and dipped. Soon it was only gravel, then dirt, then mud, then just a path beaten in the grass. The land around it got poor too, dry and rocky. And when Potchikoo got to the entrance of the Indian heaven, it was no gate of pearl, just a simple pasture gate of weathered wood. There was no one standing there to guard it, either, so he went right in.

On the other side of the gate there were no tracks, so Potchikoo walked aimlessly. All along the way, there were chokecherry bushes, not quite ripe. But Potchikoo was so hungry again that he raked them off the stems by the handful and gobbled them down, not even spitting out the pits.

The dreadful stomachaches he got, very soon, were worse than hunger, and every few steps poor Potchikoo had to relieve himself. On and on he went, day after day, eating berries to keep his strength up and staggering from the pain and shitting until he felt so weak and famished that he had to sit down. Some time went by, and then people came to sit around him. They got to talking. Someone built a fire, and soon they were roasting venison.

The taste of it made Potchikoo lonesome. Josette always fried her meat with onions.

"Well," he said, standing up when he was full, "it's time to go now."

The people didn't say good-bye though—they just laughed. There were no markers in this land, nothing but extreme and gentle emptiness. It was made to be confusing. There were no landmarks, no lookouts. The wind was strong, and the bushes grew quickly, so that every path made was instantly obscured.

But not Potchikoo's path. At regular intervals new chokecherry bushes had sprung up from the seeds that had passed through his body. So he had no trouble finding his way to the gate, out through it, and back on the road.

Potchikoo's Detour

Along the way back, he got curious and wondered what the hell for white people was like.

As he passed the pearly gates, Saint Peter was busy checking in a busload of Mormons, and so he didn't even look up and see Potchikoo take the dark fork in the road.

Walking along, Potchikoo began to think twice about what he was doing. The air felt warm and humid, and he expected it to get worse, much worse. Soon the screams of the damned would ring out and the sky would turn pitch-black. But his curiosity was, as always, stronger than his fear. He kept walking until he came to what looked like a giant warehouse.

It was a warehouse, and it was hell.

There was a little sign above the metal door marked ENTRANCE. HELL. Potchikoo got a thrill of terror in his stomach. He carefully laid his ear against the door, expecting his blood to curdle. But all he heard was the sound of rustling pages. And so, gathering his courage, he bent to the keyhole and looked in to see what it was the white race suffered.

He started back, shook his head, then bent to the keyhole again.

It was worse than flames.

They were all chained, hand and foot and even by the neck, to years and years of mail order catalogues. From the old Sears Roebuck to the Sharper Image, they were bound. Around and around the huge warehouse they dragged the heavy paper books, mumbling, collapsing from time to time to flip through the pages. Each person bent low beneath the weight. Potchikoo had always wondered where the millions of old catalogues went, and now he knew the devil gathered them, that they were instruments of torment.

The words of the damned, thin and drained, rang in his ears all the way home.

Look at that wall unit. What about this here recliner? We could put up that home gym in the basement. . . .

Potchikoo Greets Josette

On his journey through heaven and hell, Potchikoo had been a long time without sex. It was night when he finally got back home, and he could hardly wait to hold Josette in his arms. Therefore, after he had entered the house and crept up to her bed, the first words he uttered to his wife in greeting were, "Let's pitch whoopee."

Josette yelled and grabbed the swatter that she kept next to her bed to kill mosquitoes in the dark. She began to lambaste Potchikoo until she realized who it was, and that this was no awful dream.

Then they lay down in bed and had no more thoughts.

Afterward, lying there happily, Potchikoo was surprised to find that he was still passionate. They began to make love again, and still again, and over and over. At first Josette returned as good as Potchikoo gave her, but after a while it seemed that the more he made love, the more need he felt and the more heat he gave off. He was unquenchable fire.

Finally, Josette fell asleep, and let him go on and on. He was so glad to be alive again that he could never remember, afterward, how many times he had sex that night. Even he lost count. But when he woke up late the next day, Potchikoo felt a little strange, as though there was something missing. And sure enough, there was.

When Potchikoo looked under the covers, he found that his favorite part of himself was charred black and thin as a burnt twig.

Potchikoo Restored

It was terrible to have burnt his pride and joy down to nothing. It was terrible to have to face the world, especially Josette, without it. Potchikoo put his pants on and sat in the shade to think. But not until Josette left for daily Mass, and he was alone, did Potchikoo have a good idea.

He went inside and found a block of paraffin wax that Josette used to seal her jars of plum pickles. He stirred the coals in Josette's stove and melted the wax in an old coffee can. Then he dipped in his penis. It hurt the first time, but after that not so much, and then not at all. He kept dipping and dipping. It got back to the normal size, and he should have been pleased with that. But Potchikoo got grandiose ideas.

He kept dipping and dipping. He melted more wax, more and more, and kept dipping, until he was so large he could hardly stagger out the door. Luckily, the wheelbarrow was sitting in the path. He grabbed the handles and wheeled it before him into town.

There was only one road in the village then. Potchikoo went there with his wheelbarrow, calling for women. He crossed the village twice. Mothers came out in wonder, saw what was in the wheelbarrow, and whisked their daughters inside. Everybody was disgusted and scolding and indignant, except for one woman. She lived at the end of the road. Her door was always open, and she was large.

Even now, we can't use her name, this Mrs. B. No man satisfied her. But that day, Potchikoo wheeled his barrow in, and then, for once, her door was shut.

Potchikoo and Mrs. B went rolling through the house. The walls shuddered, and people standing around outside thought the whole place might collapse. Potchikoo was shaken from side to side, powerfully, as if he were on a ride at the carnival. But eventually, of course, the heat of their union softened and wilted Potchikoo back to nothing. Mrs. B was disgusted and threw him out back, into the weeds. From there he crept home to Josette, and on the crooked path he took to avoid others, he tried to think of new ways he might please her.

Potchikoo's Mean Twin

To his relief, nature returned manhood to Potchikoo in several weeks. But his troubles weren't over. One day, the tribal police appeared. They said Potchikoo had been seen stealing fence posts down the road. But they found no stolen fence posts on his property, so they did not arrest him.

More accusations were heard.

Potchikoo threw rocks at a nun, howled like a dog, and barked until she chased him off. He got drunk and tossed a pool cue out the window of the Stumble Inn. The pool cue hit the tribal chairman on the shoulder and caused a bruise. Potchikoo ran down the street laughing, flung off his clothes, ran naked through the trading store. He ripped antennas from twenty cars. He broke a portable radio that belonged to a widow, her only comfort. If a friendly dog came up to this bad Potchikoo, he lashed out with his foot. He screamed at children until tears came into their eyes, and then he knocked down the one road sign the government had seen fit to place on the reservation.

The sign was red, planted in the very middle of town, and said STOP. People were naturally proud of the sign. So, there was finally a decision to lock Potchikoo in jail, though he was dead. When the police came to get him, he went quite willingly because he was so confused.

But here's what happened.

While Potchikoo was locked up, under the eyes of the tribal sheriff, his mean twin went out and caused some mischief near the school by starting a grass fire. So now the people knew the trouble wasn't caused by Old Man Potchikoo. And next time the bad twin was seen, Josette followed him. He ran very fast, until he reached the chain link fence around the graveyard. Josette saw him jump over the fence and dodge among the stones. Then the twin got to the place where Potchikoo had been buried, lifted the ground like a lid, and wiggled under.

How Josette Takes Care of It

So the trouble was that Potchikoo had left his old body in the ground, empty, and something had found a place to live.

The people said the only thing to do was trap the mean twin and then get rid of him. But no one could agree on how to do it. People just talked and planned, no one acted. Finally Josette had to take the matter into her own hands.

One day she made a big pot of stew, and into it she put a bird. Into the roasted bird, Josette put a bit of blue plaster that had fallen off the Blessed Virgin's robe while she cleaned the altar. She took the stew and left the whole pot just outside the cemetery fence. From her hiding place deep in a lilac bush, she saw the mean twin creep forth. He took the pot in his hands and gulped down every morsel, then munched the bird up, bones and all. Stuffed full, he lay down to sleep. He snored. After a while, he woke and looked around himself, very quietly. That was when Josette came out of the bush.

"In the name of the Holy Mother of God!" she cried. "Depart!"

So the thing stepped out of Potchikoo's old body, all hairless and smooth and wet and gray. But Josette had no pity. She pointed sternly at the dark stand of pines, where no one went, and slowly, with many a sigh and backward look, the thing walked over there.

Potchikoo's old body lay, crumpled like a worn suit of clothes, where the thing had stepped out. Right there, Josette made a fire, a little fire. When the blaze was very hot, she threw in the empty skin. It crackled in the flames, shed sparks, and was finally reduced to a crisp of ashes, which Josette brushed carefully into a little sack, and saved in her purse.

Saint Potchikoo

With his old body burnt, Potchikoo existed in his spiritual flesh. Yet having been to the other side of life and back, he wasn't sure where he belonged. Sometimes he found his heaven with Josette, sometimes he longed for the pasture gate. He became certain that the end of his living days was near, and he felt sorry for himself. He was also very jealous when it came to Josette, and convinced that old men were in love with her, just waiting for him to croak. Therefore, he decided to have himself stuffed and placed in a corner of their bedroom, where he could keep an eye on his widow. He told her of his plan.

"That way, you'll never forget me," he crooned in a pathetic voice.

"I'll never forget you anyway," said Josette. "Who the hell could?"

Potchikoo sought out a taxidermist in a neighboring town, the sort of person who mounted prize walleyes and the heads of buck deer.

"What about me?" said Potchikoo.

"What about you?" said the taxidermist.

"I'd like to get stuffed," said Potchikoo.

"You must be dead first," said the professional.

Oh yes, Potchikoo had forgotten this. Dead first. How to accomplish that? He considered this obstacle as he walked back to his house. Death. Potchikoo thought harder. At last, another option presented itself. Potchikoo decided to spend his golden years carving a lifelike statue of Potchikoo from the tall stump of an old oak tree right outside the door. Thus, once he was gone, he would watch over his love and present a forbidding sight to any akiwenzii who came to court her. Delighted with his notion, he began carving the very same day.

Months passed, a year passed, and Potchikoo's statue became a legend. His project, begun in jealousy, became through rumor a sign of enormous grace. Divine light had descended on a habitual miscreant. Talk was that the old rascal had converted and was carving the Virgin Mary, or maybe Saint Joseph, or perhaps again the people's own Blessed Kateri, right in his front yard. Potchikoo put up a canvas screen and worked there every single day. The wrenching sound of his chisel and the tapping of his mallet could be heard at any time, but he allowed no glimpse of his masterwork. He gave no interviews. Just kept working. Not until the statue was finished did he speak, and then it was only a notice of the unveiling. Which would occur on Easter morning.

At least a hundred people gathered after Mass, and another hundred were there already, waiting for the canvas that surrounded the statue to drop. Potchikoo was very pleased, and made a most glorious speech. The speech was long, and very satisfying to Potchikoo, and at the end of it he suddenly pulled the cord that held the curtain before the statue.

Silence. There was a lot of silence from the people. Potchikoo interpreted their silence as awe, and for sure, he felt the awe of it too. For the statue of himself had all of his unmistakable features, including the fantasy of his favorite part of himself at its most commanding. Those who were religious shook their heads and quickly left. Those who weren't, but who had good taste, left as well. That left only the pagans with bad taste to admire what they saw, but that was enough for Potchikoo. He considered his project a success. During the years of quiet happiness that followed with Josette he never mislaid his hat, as there was a place to hang it right beside the door.

The Butcher's Wife

The Butcher's Wife

1

Once, my braids swung heavy as ropes.
Men feared them like the gallows.
Night fell
When I combed them out.
No one could see me in the dark.

Then I stood still
Too long and the braids took root.
I wept, so helpless.
The braids tapped deep and flourished.

A man came by with an ox on his shoulders.
He yoked it to my apron
And pulled me from the ground.
From that time on I wound the braids around my head
So that my arms would be free to tend him.

2

He could lift a grown man by the belt with his teeth.
In a contest, he'd press a whole hog, a side of beef.

He loved his highballs, his herring, and the attentions of women.
He died pounding his chest with no last word for anyone.

The gin vessels in his face broke and darkened. I traced them
Far from that room into Bremen on the Sea.
The narrow streets twisted down to the piers.
And far off, in the black, rocking water, the lights of trawlers
Beckoned, like the heart's uncertain signals,
Faint, and final.

3

Of course I planted a great, full bush of roses on his grave.
Who else would give the butcher roses but his wife?
Each summer, I am reminded of the heart surging from his vest,
Mocking all the high stern angels
By pounding for their spread skirts.

The flowers unfurl, offering themselves,
And I hear his heart pound on the earth like a great fist,
Demanding another round of the best wine in the house.
Another round, he cries, and another round all summer long,
Until the whole damn world reels toward winter drunk.

That Pull from the Left

Butch once remarked to me how sinister it was
alone, after hours, in the dark of the shop
to find me there hunched over two weeks' accounts
probably smoked like a bacon from all those Pall-Malls.

Odd comfort when the light goes, the case lights left on
and the rings of baloney, the herring, the parsley,
arranged in the strict, familiar ways.

Whatever intactness holds animals up
has been carefully taken, what's left are the parts.
Just look in the cases, all counted and stacked.

Step-and-a-Half Waleski used to come to the shop
and ask for the cheap cut, she would thump, sniff, and finger.
This one too old. This one here for my supper.
Two days and you do notice change in the texture.

I have seen them the day before slaughter.
Knowing the outcome from the moment they enter
the chute, the eye rolls, blood is smeared on the lintel.
Mallet or bullet they lunge toward their darkness.

But something queer happens when the heart is delivered.
When a child is born, sometimes the left hand is stronger.
You can train it to fail, still the knowledge is there.
That is the knowledge in the hand of a butcher

that adds to its weight. Otto Kröger could fell
a dray horse with one well-placed punch to the jaw,
and yet it is well known how thorough he was.

He never sat down without washing his hands,
and he was a maker, his sausage was *echt*
so that even Waleski had little complaint.
Butch once remarked there was no one so deft
as my Otto. So true, there is great tact involved
in parting the flesh from the bones that it loves.

How we cling to the bones. Each joint is a web
of small tendons and fibers. He knew what I meant
when I told him I felt something pull from the left,
and how often it clouded the day before slaughter.

Something queer happens when the heart is delivered.

The Carmelites

They're women, not like me but like the sun
burning cold on a winter afternoon,
audacious brilliance from a severe height,
living in the center as the town revolves
around them in a mess. Of course
we want to know what gives behind their fence,
behind the shades, the yellow brick
convent huge in the black green pines.
We pass it, every one of us, on rounds
we make our living at. There's one
I've spoken to. Tall, gaunt, and dressed in brown,
her office is to fetch the mail, pay bills,
and fasten wheat into the Virgin's arms.
I've thought of her, so ordinary, rising every night,
scarred like the moon in her observance,
shaved and bound and bandaged
in rough blankets like a poor mare's carcass,
muttering for courage at the very hour
cups crack in the cupboards downstairs, and Otto
turns to me with urgency and power.
Tremendous love, the cry stuffed back, the statue
smothered in its virtue till the glass corrodes,
and the buried structure shows,
the hoops, the wires, the blackened arcs,
freeze to acid in the strange heart.

Clouds

The furnace is stoked. I'm loaded
on gin. One bottle in the clinkers
hidden since spring
when Otto took the vow
and ceremoniously poured
the rotgut, the red-eye, the bootlegger's brew
down the scoured steel sink,
overcoming the reek
of oxblood.
That was one promise he kept.
He died two weeks after, not a drop crossed his lips
in the meantime. I know
now he kept some insurance,
one bottle at least
against his own darkness.
I'm here, anyway, to give it some use.

From the doorway the clouds pass me through.
The town stretches to fields. The six avenues
crossed by seventeen streets,
the tick, tack, and toe
of boxes and yards
settle into the dark.

Dogs worry their chains.
Men call to their mothers
and finish. The women sag into the springs.
What kind of thoughts, Mary Kröger, are these?
With a headful of spirits,
how else can I think?
Under so many clouds,
such hooded and broken
old things. They go on
simply folding, unfolding, like sheets
hung to dry and forgotten.

And no matter how careful I watch them,
they take a new shape,
escaping my concentrations,
they slip and disperse
and extinguish themselves.
They melt before I half unfathom their forms.
Just as fast, a few bones
disconnecting beneath us.
It is too late, I fear, to call these things back.
Not in this language.
Not in this life.

I know it. The tongue is unhinged by the sauce.
But these clouds, creeping toward us
each night while the milk

gets scorched in the pan,
great soaked loaves of bread
are squandering themselves in the west.

Look at them: Proud, unpausing.
Open and growing, we cannot destroy them
or stop them from moving
down each avenue,
the dogs turn on their chains,
children feel through the windows.
What else should we feel our way through—

We lay our streets over
the deepest cries of the earth
and wonder why everything comes down to this:
The days pile and pile.
The bones are too few
and too foreign to know.
Mary, you do not belong here at all.

Sometimes I take back in tears this whole town.
Let everything be how it could have been, once:
a land that was empty and perfect as clouds.
But this is the way people are.
All that appears to us empty,
We fill.
What is endless and simple,
We carve, and initial,

and narrow
roads plow through the last of the hills
where our gravestones rear small
black vigilant domes.
Our friends, our family, the dead of our wars
deep in this strange earth
we want to call ours.

Shelter

My four adopted sons in photographs
wear solemn black. Their faces comprehend
their mother's death, an absence in a well
of empty noise, and Otto strange and lost.
Her name was Mary also, Mary Kröger.
Two of us have lived and one is gone.
Her hair was blond; it floated back in wings,
and still you see her traces in the boys:
bright hair and long, thin, knotted woman's hands.
I knew her, Mary Kröger, and we were bosom friends.
All graves are shelters for our mislaid twins.

Otto was for many years her husband,
and that's the way I always thought of him.
I nursed her when she sickened and the cure
fell through at Rochester. The healing bath
that dropped her temperature, I think, too fast.
I was in attendance at her death:
She sent the others out. She rose and gripped my arm
and tried to make me promise that I'd care
for Otto and the boys. I had to turn away
as my own mother had when her time came.
How few do not return in memory

and make us act in ways we can't explain.
I could not lie to ease her, living, dying.
All graves are full of such accumulation.

And yet, the boys were waiting in New York
to take the first boat back to Otto's folks
in Germany, prewar, dark powers were at work,
and Otto asked me on the westbound bus
to marry him. I could not tell him no—
We help our neighbors out. I loved him though

It took me several years to know I did
from that first time he walked in to deliver
winter food. Through Father Adler's kitchen,
he shouldered half an ox like it was bread
and looked at me too long for simple greeting.
This is how our live complete themselves,
as effortless as weather, circles blaze
in ordinary days, and through our waking selves
they reach, to touch our true and sleeping speech.

So I took up with Otto, took the boys
and watched for them, and made their daily bread
from what the grocer gave them in exchange
for helping him. It's hard to tell you how
they soon became so precious I got sick
from worry, and woke up for two months straight

and had to check them, sleeping, in their beds
and had to watch and see each breathe or move
before I could regain my sleep again.
All graves are pregnant with our nearest kin.

The Slow Sting of Her Company

Otto brought one sister from that town
they never talk about. His father shook
one great red fist, a bludgeon, in the air
behind them as dry sparks released the wheels.
I pictured him, still standing there, now shrunk—
a carved root pickling in its own strong juice.
They speak his name and wipe it from their lips.
                  Proud Hilda hides his picture
                  in a drawer with underskirts.

Tall Hilda sniffed and twisted that gold chain
my Otto gave her. Other, lesser men
have gifted her with more impressive things.
She keeps them in a drawer with towels and sheets.
I came upon a sentimental locket,
embossed with words, initials interfixed
within the breasts of dour, molting swans.
                  Proud Hilda cracked it open,
                  smiled, and clicked it shut.

How many men had begged her heavy hand
I do not know. I think I loved her too
in ways that I am not sure how to tell—

I reached one day to gather back her hair:
wild marigold. I touched one hidden ear
and drew my fingers, burning, from the stone
that swung a cold light from the polished lobe.
                    Tall Hilda took my hand in hers and kissed
                    the palm, and closed that mark inside my fist.

She lived alone and thickened in that town,
refusing company for weeks on end.
We left food at her door; she took it in;
her dull lamp deepened as the night wore on.
I went to her when everything was wrong.
We sat all evening talking children, men.
She laughed at me, and said it was my ruin.
                    My giving till I dropped.
                    Live blood let down the drain.

I never let her know how those words cut
me serious—her questioning my life. One night
a slow thing came, provoked by weariness,
to cram itself up every slackened nerve;
as if my body were a whining hive
and each cell groaning with a sweet, thick lead—
I turned and struck at Otto in our bed;
all night, all night the poison, till I swarmed
                    back empty to his cold
                    and dreaming arms.

Here Is a Good Word for
Step-and-a-Half Waleski

At first we all wondered what county or town
she had come from. Quite soon it was clear to us all
that was better unquestioned, and better unknown.
Who wanted to hear what had happened or failed
to occur. Why the dry wood had not taken fire.
Much less, why the dogs were unspeakably disturbed

when she ground the cold cinders that littered our walk
with her run-to-ground heels. That Waleski approached
with a swiftness uncommon for one of her age.
Even spiders spun clear of her lengthening shadow.
Her headlong occurrence unnerved even Otto
who wrapped up the pork rinds like they were glass trinkets
and saluted her passage with a good stiff drink.

But mine is a good word for Step-and-a-Half Waleski.
Scavenger, bone picker, lived off our alleys
when all we threw out were the deadliest scrapings
from licked-over pots. And even that hurt.
And for whatever one of us laughed in her face,
at least two prayed in secret, went home half afraid
of that mirror, what possible leavings they'd find there.

But mine is a good word, and even that hurts.
A rhyme-and-a-half for a woman of parts,
because someone must pare the fruit soft to the core
into slivers, must wrap the dead bones in her skirts
and lay these things out on her table, and fit
each oddment to each to resemble a life.

Portrait of the Town Leonard

I thought I saw him look my way and crossed
my breast before I could contain myself.
Beneath those glasses, thick as lead-barred windows,
his eyes ran through his head, the double barrels
of an old gun, sick on its load, the trigger held
in place by one thin metal bow.

Going toward the Catholic church, whose twin
white dunce caps speared the clouds for offerings,
we had to pass him on the poured stone bridge.
For nickels we could act as though we'd not
been offered stories. How these all turned out
we knew, each one, just how the river eats
within its course the line of reasoning.

He went, each morning, to the first confession.
The sulking curtains bit their lips behind him.
Still those in closer pews could hear the sweet
and limber sins he'd made up on the spot.
I saw a few consider, and take note—
procedural. They'd try them out at home.

And once, a windless August, when the sun
released its weight and all the crops were burned,

he kept watch as the river thickened. Land
grew visibly and reeked to either side,
till windowed hulks, forgotten death cars reared
where dark fish leapt, and gaped, and snatched the air.

Leonard Commits Redeeming Adulteries
with All the Women in Town

When I take off my glasses, these eyes are dark magnets
that draw the world into my reach.
First the needles, as I walk the quiet streets,
work their way from the cushions of dust.
The nails in the rafters twist laboriously out
and the oven doors drop
an inch open.
The sleep smell of yesterday's baking
rises in the mouth.
A good thing.

The street lamps wink off just at dawn,
still they bend their stiff necks like geese drinking.
My vision is drinking in the star-littered lawn.
When the porch ivy weaves to me—
Now is the time.
Women put down their coffee cups, all over town.
Men drift down the sidewalks, thinking,
What did she want?
But it is too late for husbands.
Their wives do not question
what it is that dissolves
all reserve. Why they suddenly think of cracked Leonard.

They uncross themselves, forsaking
all protection. They long to be opened and known
because the secret is perishable, kept, and desire
in love with its private ruin.
I open my hands and they come to me, now.
In our palms dark instructions that cannot be erased,
only followed, only known along the way.

And it is right, oh women of the town, it is *right*.
Your mouths, like the seals of important documents
break for me, destroying the ring's raised signature,
the cracked edges melting to mine.

Unexpected Dangers

I'm much the worse for wear, it's double true.
Too many incidents
a man might misconstrue—
my conduct, for a lack of innocence.

I seem to get them crazed or lacking sense
in the first place.
Ancient, solid gents
I sit by on the bus because they're safe,

get me coming, going, with their canes,
or what is worse,
the spreading stains
across the seat. I recognize at once

just what they're up to, rustling in their coats.
There was a priest,
the calmer sort,
his cassock flowing down from neck to feet.

We got to talking, and I brushed his knee
by accident,
and dutifully,
he took my hand and put it back

not quite where it belonged; his judgment
was not that exact.
I underwent
a kind of odd conversion from his act.

They do call minds like mine one-track.
One track is all you need
to understand
their loneliness, then bite the hand that feeds

upon you, in a terrible blind grief.

My Name Repeated on the Lips of the Dead

Last night, my dreams were full of Otto's best friends.
I sat in the kitchen, wiping the heavy silver,
and listened to the losses, tough custom, and fouled accounts
of the family bootlegger, county sheriff:
Rudy J. V. Jacklitch, who sat just beside me,
wiping his wind-cracked hands
with lard smeared on a handkerchief.

Our pekinese-poodle went and darkened his best wool trousers,
and he leapt up, yelling for a knife!

These are the kinds of friends
I had to tend in those days:
great, thick men, devouring
Fleisch, Spaetzle, the very special
potato salad for which I dice
onions so fine they are invisible.

Rudy J. V. Jacklitch was a bachelor, but he cared
for his mother, a small spider of a woman—all fingers.
She covered everything, from the kettle to the radio,
with a doily. The whole house
dripped with lace, frosting fell
from each surface in fantastic shapes.

When Otto died, old Rudy came by
with a couple jugs for the mourners' supper.
He stayed on past midnight, every night the month after
he would bring me a little something
to put the night away.

After a short while I knew his purpose.
His glance slipped as the evening
and the strong drink wore on.
Playing cribbage I always won,
a sure sign he was distracted.
I babbled like a talking bird,
never let him say the words
I knew were in him.

Then one night he came by,
already loaded to the gills,
rifle slung in the back window
of his truck: *Going out*
to shoot toads. He was peeved
with me. I'd played him all wrong.
He said his mother *knew just what I was.*

The next thing I heard that blurred night
was that Rudy drove his light truck
through the side of a barn,
and that among the living
he stayed long enough

to pronounce my name, like a curse
through the rage and foam of his freed blood.

So I was sure, for a time and a time after,
that Rudy carried
my name down to hell on his tongue
like a black coin.

I would wake, in the deepest of places,
and hear my name called.
My name like a strange new currency they read:
Mary Kröger
with its ring of the authentic
when dropped
or struck between their fingers.

How I feared to have it whispered in their mouths!

Mary Kröger
growing softer and thinner
till it dissolved
like a wafer under all that polishing.

A Mother's Hell

The Widow Jacklitch

All night, all night, the cat wants out again.
I've locked her in the kitchen where she tears
From wall to wall. Her bullet head leaves marks;
She swings from tablecloths, dislodges pots.
When Rudy was alive the cat was all
You ever could have wanted in a child, it sat so still
And diligently sucked its whiskers clean. I cram
A doily in my mouth to still the scream.

All night the sweethearts dandle in the weeds.
It's terrible, the little bleats they make
Outside my window. Girls not out of braids
Walk by. I see their fingers hike their skirts
Way up their legs. I say it's dirt.
The cat's got rubbage on her brain
As well. She backs on anything that's stiff.
I try to keep the pencils out of reach.

That Kröger widow practiced what she'd preach
A mile a minute. If she was a cat
I'd drown her in a tub of boiling fat
And nail her up like suet, out in back

Where birds fly down to take their chance.
I don't like things with beaks. I don't
like anything that makes a beating sound.

Beat, beat, all night they hammered at the truck
With bats. But he had locked himself
In stubbornly as when a boy; I'd knock
Until my knuckles scabbed and bled
And blue paint scraped into the wounds. He'd laugh
Behind his door. I'd hear him pant and thrill.
A mother's hell. But I'd feel the good blindness stalk
Us together. Son and mother world without end forever.

Rudy Comes Back

I knew at once, when the lights dimmed.
He was pissing on the works.
The generator fouled a beat
and recovered.
My doors were locked
anyway, and the big white dog
unchained in the yard.

Outside, the wall of hollyhocks
raved for mercy from the wind's strap.
The valves of the roses opened,
so sheltering his step
with their frayed mouths.

I don't know how he entered
the dull bitch at my feet.
She rose in a nightmare's hackles,
glittering, shedding heat
from her mild eyes.

All night we kept watch,
never leaving the white-blue ring
of the kitchen. I could hear him out there,
scratching in the porch hall, cold

and furtive as a cat in winter.
Toward dawn I got the gun.

And he was out there, Rudy J. V. Jacklitch,
the bachelor who drove his light truck
through the side of a barn on my account.
He'd lost flesh. The gray skin of his face dragged.
His clothes were bunched.

He stood reproachful,
in one hand the wooden board
and the pegs, still my crib.
In the other the ruined bouquet
of larkspur I wouldn't take.

I was calm. This was something I'd foreseen.
After all, he took my name down to hell,
a thin black coin.
Repeatedly, repeatedly, to his destruction,
he called.
And I had not answered then.
And I would not answer now.

The flowers chafed to flames of dust in his hands.
The earth drew the wind in like breath and held on.
But I did not speak
or cry out
until the dawn, until the confounding light.

New Vows

The night was clean as the bone of a rabbit blown hollow.
I cast my hood of dogskin
away, and my shirt of nettles.
Ten years had been enough. I left my darkened house.

The trick was in living that death to its source.
When it happened, I wandered toward more than I was.

Widowed by men, I married the dark firs,
as if I were walking in sleep toward their arms.
I drank, without fear or desire,
this odd fire.

Now shadows move freely within me as words.
These are eternal, these stunned, loosened verbs.
And I can't tell you yet
how truly I belong

to the hiss and shift of wind,
these slow, variable mouths
through which, at certain times, I speak in tongues.

The Seven Sleepers

Fooling God

I must become small and hide where he cannot reach.
I must become dull and heavy as an iron pot.
I must be tireless as rust and bold as roots
growing through the locks on doors
and crumbling the cinder blocks
of the foundations of his everlasting throne.
I must be strange as pity so he'll believe me.
I must be terrible and brush my hair
so that he finds me attractive.
Perhaps if I invoke Clare, the patron saint of television.
Perhaps if I become the images
passing through the cells of a woman's brain.

I must be very large and block his sight.
I must be sharp and impetuous as knives.
I must insert myself into the bark of his apple trees,
and cleave the bones of his cows. I must be the marrow
that he drinks into his cloud-wet body.
I must be careful and laugh when he laughs.
I must turn down the covers and guide him in.
I must fashion his children out of Play-Doh, blue, pink, green.
I must pull them from between my legs
and set them before the television.

I must hide my memory in a mustard grain
so that he'll search for it over time until time is gone.
I must lose myself in the world's regard and disparagement.
I must remain this person and be no trouble.
None at all. So he'll forget.
I'll collect dust out of reach,
a single dish from a set, a flower made of felt,
a tablet the wrong shape to choke on.

I must become essential and file everything
under my own system,
so we can lose him and his proofs and adherents.
I must be a doubter in a city of belief
that hails his signs (the great footprints
long as limousines, the rough print on the wall).
On the pavement where his house begins
fainting women kneel. I'm not among them
although they polish the brass tongues of his lions
with their own tongues
and taste the everlasting life.

The Sacraments

1 Baptism

As the sun dancers, in their helmets of sage,
stopped at the sun's apogee
and stood in the waterless light,
so, after loss, it came to this:
that for each year the being was destroyed,
I was to sacrifice a piece of my flesh.
The keen knife hovered
and the skin flicked in the bowl.
Then the sun, the life that consumes us,
burst into agony.

We began, the wands and the head crowns of sage,
the feathers cocked over our ears.
When the bird joined the circle and called,
we cried back, shrill breath
through the bones in our teeth.
Her wings closed over us, her dark red
claws drew us upward by the scars,
so that we hung by the flesh

as in the moment before birth
when the spirit is quenched

in whole pain, suspended
until there is no choice, the body
slams to earth,
the new life starts.

2 Communion

It is spring. The tiny frogs pull
their strange new bodies out
of the suckholes, the sediment of rust,
and float upward, each in a silver bubble
that breaks on the water's surface
to one clear unceasing note of need.

Sometimes, when I hear them,
I leave our bed and stumble
among the white shafts of weeds
to the edge of the pond.
I sink to the throat,
and witness the ravenous trill
of the body transformed at last and then consumed
in a rush of music.

Sing to me, sing to me.
I *have never been so cold*
rising out of sleep.

3 Confirmation

I was twelve, in my body
three eggs were already marked
for the future.
Two golden, one dark.
And the man,
he was selected from other men,
by a blow on the cheek
similar to mine.
That is how we knew,
from the first meeting.
There was no question.
There was the wound.

4 Matrimony

It was frightening, the trees in their rigid postures
using up the sun,
as the earth tilted its essential degree.
Snow covered everything. Its confusing glare
doubled the view
so that I saw you approach
my empty house
not as one man, but as a landscape
repeating along the walls of every room
papering over the cracked grief.

I knew as I stepped into the design,
as I joined the chain of hands,
and let the steeple of fire
be raised above our heads.
We had chosen the costliest pattern,
the strangest, the most enduring.
We were afraid as we stood between the willows,
as we shaped the standard words with our tongues.
Then it was done. The scenery multiplied
around us and we turned.
We stared calmly from the pictures.

5 Penance

I am sorry I ruined the oatmeal
which must remain in the bowl. Sorry
my breath hardened on the carpet and the slashed fur
climbed, raving, off the wall.
I am sorry for the ominous look, for using tears.
Sorry for the print on the page,
for wearing the shoes of a dead woman
bought at a yard sale.
She still walks, walks
restlessly, treading the mill. I am
sorry I could not lift out the stain
with powerful enzymes, with spit, with vinegar.
Sorry I pickled your underwear
and froze my hands to the knob
so that you had to turn me to gain entrance
to the kingdom without spots or wrinkles.
I am sorry I have failed so I am not allowed
to leave the table, to which my knees are strapped.
Sorry I cannot leave you behind. For you are mine.
You are everything. And I am sorry.

6 Holy Orders

God, I was not meant to be the isolate
cry in this body.
I was meant to have your tongue in my mouth.

That is why I stand by your great plaster lips
waiting for your voice to unfold from its dark slot.

Your hand clenched in the shape of a bottle.
Your mouth painted shut on the answer.
Your eyes, two blue mirrors, in which I am perfectly denied.

I open my mouth and I speak
though it is only a thin sound, a leaf
scraping on a leaf.

7 Extreme Unction

When the blue steam stalls over the land
and the resinous apples
turn to mash, then to a cider whose thin
twang shrivels the tongue,
the snakes hatch
twirling from the egg.

In the shattered teacup, from the silvering
boards of the barn,
in the heat of rotting mulch hay,
they soak up the particles of light

so that all winter
welded in the iron sheath
of sludge under the pond
they continue, as we do,
drawing closer to the source,
their hearts beating slower
as the days narrow
until there is this one pale aperture
and the tail sliding through

then the systole, the blackness of heaven.

The Seven Sleepers

Seven Christian youths of Ephesus, according to legend, hid themselves in a cave in A.D. 250 to escape persecution for their faith. They fell asleep in the cave, their youthfulness was miraculously preserved, and they were discovered by accident some two hundred years later. The Seven Sleepers are the patron saints of insomniacs.

Wandering without sleep I looked for God
and found this moment to praise.

Come with me, impossible night.
I am moving bitterly and far away.
Over vast and open country pulsing with dead light,
over the atomic voids
onto the great plains in massed vapor
in the tumble fever of my dreams,
I seek you,
Nameless one. My god, my leaf.

I seek you in the candles of pine and in the long tongue
furled in sleep. I seek you in the August suspension
of leaves as steps of sunlight
tottering through air.
Drunk beneath the overpass at dawn
passed out in a Hefty bag.
On the hills, the tyrant moon,

and in the faces of my daughters,
I seek you driving prayerfully
as a member of the Sacred Heart Driving Club.
I seek you in the headless black wings of the vulture
Motionless dial, my death.

I seek you full of me, as if I could drink you in
and overcome myself.
I seek you under everything
in parallel faults and shifting plates.
Deadened to myself in the morning
and in the flat thumb of day
I seek you balancing the hammer.
I seek you naked, holding red stones,
as I walk beneath the torn sky, toward home,
where I open my throat to the black river
of my fears, all my fears.
You are faceless in the twig cells dividing upward.
Always to the light.
You lie buried with me twenty days and nights
without a candle, breathing through a straw
and the air is sweet, clear, like food.
From our grave, we can smell the leaves and water,
taste sunlight, taste the chemical structure of night.

I seek you, I find you everywhere, in the white day,
and in the relentless throat call
of physical love.

Our bodies in winter, our skin dry as paper,
we are stroking the urgent message
written in the subskin, the rat-brain, subcortex,
written there in lemon juice that heat of touch
turns visible, written in the print
of a child detective.

Dragging a cart of splinters,
tin nailed to the soles of your feet,
you walk over me. You strike flame from my body.
I burn at the magnetic center as the leaves fall
steps of fire
leading down into the earth.

I find you in my newborn child,
harnessed to my breasts with cotton, small and molten.
Her need for me as pure as my need for you.

I find you in the miraculous dung of the horned beetle
which cures the heart of anguish
I find you in the ash I must become melting in the rain,
new rain, descending.
Call me, speak from the water
lit by spilled oils
Sing to me from the mouth of the fish artfully arranged
on smashed ice.
Sing from the empty seas.

Behind us, before us,
in all things now I praise you.
Gold One. Prime Mover. Boring Prima Facie.
I praise you in Jack Daniel's at the foot of the bed
and in the isolation of this dream.

Thing of holes, thing of lies, thing of shoulder pads,
thing of beautiful smashed mouth
thing of drenched fabric,
thing unmade by woman in her own body:
I fall face down into the sweet slab of cake
into the roaring flesh, licking crumbs off you
Face down in the yard, in the dust of sexual heat.
I praise you.

In the word
and in the void between words.
You are the pause, the synaptic skip.
You are the meaning between the syllables.
Walking up the water drops until I reach the cloud,
Walking up the leaves
until the crown of the tree is massed
like a cloak around me. Following snow
to the place of snow,
of course I praise you,
there is nothing else,
there is no other task.

When I first began listening to your voice I was huge,
I was a child.
I sat in the ash tree as light froze in the sky
and willed you to leave the kitchen.
Then, suddenly, you were around me in the leaves.
I thought there was laughter in the hissing wind
and I was afraid, I saw
my name written on the dark surface.

Gold One. Mother. Boring Prima Facie.
You and I are dust of cellular radiance,
of intricacy and rushing noise.
Hammer of time, hammer of love.
You rise in the bones of my husband.
You fall in the hands of the silver clock.
You fly off the grasses and you seed the water.
I praise you in the old red-brick house of my childhood
crumbling to rose,
to silver, to agate, to sludge.

Black tar. Deep tar. Cozening preserver.
Steep cliff ignited in the halo
as the sun tips its hood of fire.
I praise you in the cicatrix of sex
and the brilliant umbilical happiness
of sleek, heavy snakes
twining and untwining in the grass.

I praise you in my iron shoes,
magnetized and grounding me.
I praise you in my shoes forged of steam,
in my shoes of dripping felt, my shoes of bottle caps,
my garbage shoes, my shoes of wood ash and velvet,
my uncomplaining shoes, my whore's shoes
that set me above you.
I praise you underneath me, walking,
my reflection in the unreflecting ground,
moving below me through dirt and ledge.
My twin of the grave.
My death glove. My other.
I praise you in the longing of my infant,
in my children, whom I have brought here to search you out,
who have begun, already, starting with my own face.

God, I have killed you in myself
again, again, dragging you to light by the tail,
I have hammered you to one thin ribbon.
Now I release you!
Blue and coiling in the simple world.

I praise you in the power of these words
to seize your image, to abandon mine.
Every motion of your dance is the dance
of my daily life, and yet you hide yourself.
I praise you in the roaring veil.

How weak I have become walking in my heavy shoes.
You will have to lift me, you will have to be my body.
There is only one perfect love, that between
an infant and its protector.
All else is magical failure.

I sift my thoughts into this perfect zero,
into the silken core between minus and plus.
I walk through the terminal number
backward, into the negative
where deep snow falls.
Again I am a child. I stand in the snow
and all around me is the snow
I stand there until I turn to snow.
And then, for a moment, I know you.

You were made by women.
You were made because we needed someone,
a man, to blame.
You were struck from our hands
and kneaded to your man-shape like dough
Then you rose and rose and doubled to enclose us
in the God-shape, the myth.

Perfect light, manuscript of ions, come toward me.
Advance, shaking, futile.
I remember.
After the rape I went to my chair.

I sat, looking at the carpet.
I felt the angel of forgiveness unfurl her iron wings.
Her feathers ripped through my back like razors
Now, when I close my wings over you—
Know how it is to be a woman,
to fight your way out of the body
only to be cast between the ribs of a man again.

Light of my brain burning day and night,
I praise you as a driver loses the road
in snow and drives across the fields
of snow, the snow absolving human presence.
Star. Failing light. I praise you,
as I'm sitting here, praise you fervently,
and without hope, every day.

The first waves rushed in, immaculate and foaming.
The child was given up to love.
Pressed deeply against the sound of the world,
she breathed the dark spores
of earth, slept underneath the twelve-branched heart.

Let us go down into the earth every night.
Let us bite down,
let us chew the bitter wood to paste
as deer in their winter yards circulate, stripping
everything into themselves
until they drift out,
in spring, wise and ravenous.

I lie down in the grass, watching, and when the coyote turns
her ass to the wind, looks at me across her shoulder,
that is when we regard each other,
as the snow bleeds white around the base of Sweetgrass.

You are everything. There is nowhere
I do not praise you.
In bed, in the body.
You rise toward me in the bones
of my wife, my husband, my lover.
Paging through the white flesh, the black, the brown,
which we wear as we dance the skin dance
Someone please!
Remove my beer-can vest, my skin of vinyl sheet music!
Speak from the water, speak from the fucking.
I praise you in the body out of the body.
Ash I must become in new rain descending.
Child, dear raven's heart, new messenger.

Hammer of love, hammer of time,
self I've killed you in myself,
again, again, dragging you to light by the tail,
pounding you to one thin ribbon.
Now I release you,
blue and coiling in the simple world.

How sad I have become walking in my heavy shoes.
You will have to kill me, you will have to be my body.
Our love like all love is magical failure.

Perfect light, manuscript of ions.
I write your praises
on my own skin
with the stylus of a sharpened nail.

I wake in the blue hours once again,
my whole life spilling through me,
as loons pour
the cold green tea of their laughter
across the rose-slabbed lakes of Ontario.
I am one thing. I am nothing you can name.
I pray in the woods, begging to be taken,
the way leaves and stones are
whirled into your rushing mouth.

River of snow, river of twinned carp,
Sky of three holes, sky of white paper.
I praise you the way shadows
of deer move beyond the cut lawn
stripping everything into them, flowers, bark,
the frail blossoms of the poke, the weeds,
yew trees, cedar, lythrum, tender new labia of phlox.
Shadow of my need, shadow of hunger,
shadow infinite and made of gesture,
my god, my leaf,
graceful, ravenous, moving in endless circles
as the sweet seeds hang waxen yellow in the maple.

Avila

Teresa of Avila's brother, Rodrigo, emigrated to America in 1535 and died
in a fight with Natives on the banks of the Rio de la Plata.

      —Footnote to The Life of Teresa of
       Jesus, translated and edited by
       E. Allison Peers

Sister, do you remember our cave of stones,
how we entered from the white heat of afternoons,
chewed seeds, and plotted one martyrdom
more cruel than the last?
You threw your brown hair back
and sang Pax Vobiscum to the imaginary guard,
a leopard on the barge of Ignatius.
Now I see you walking toward me, discalced like the poor,
as the dogwood trees come into blossom.
Their centers are the wounds of nails,
deep and ragged. The spears of heaven
bristle along the path you take,
turning me aside.

Dear sister, as the mountain grows out of the air,
as the well of fresh water
is sunk in the grinding sea,

as the castle within rises stone upon stone,
I still love you. But that is only
the love of a brother for a sister, after all,
and God has nothing to do with it.

Saint Clare

She refused to marry when she was twelve and was so impressed by a Lenten sermon of Saint Francis in 1212 that she ran away from her home in Assisi, received her habit, and took the vow of absolute poverty. Since Francis did not yet have a convent for women, he placed her in the Benedictine convent near Basia, where she was joined by her younger sister, Agnes. Her father sent twelve armed men to bring Agnes back, but Clare's prayers rendered her so heavy they were unable to budge her.

—John H. Delaney,
Pocket Dictionary of Saints

1 The Call

First I heard the voice throbbing across the river.
I saw the white phosphorescence of his robe.
As he stepped from the boat, as he walked
there spread from each footfall a black ripple,
from each widening ring a wave,
from the waves a sea that covered the moon.
So I was seized in total night
and I abandoned myself in his garment
like a fish in a net. The slip knots
tightened on me and I rolled
until the sudden cry hauled me out.

Then this new element, a furnace of mirrors,
in which I watch myself burn.
The scales of my old body melt away like coins,
for I was rich, once, and my father
had already chosen my husband.

2 Before

I kept my silver rings in a box of porphyrite.
I ate salt on bread. I could sew.
I could mend the petals of a rose.
My nipples were pink, my sister's brown.
In the fall we filled our wide skirts with walnuts
for our mother to crack with a wooden hammer.
She put the whorled meats into our mouths,
closed our lips with her finger
and said Hush. So we slept
and woke to find our bodies arching into bloom.
It happened to me first,
the stain on the linen, the ceremonial
seal which was Eve's fault.
In the church at Assisi I prayed. I listened
to Brother Francis and I took his vow.
The embroidered decorations at my bodice
turned real, turned to butterflies and were dispersed.
The girdle of green silk, the gift from my father
slithered from me like a vine,
so I was something else that grew from air,
and I was light, the skeins of hair
that my mother had divided with a comb of ivory
were cut from my head and parceled to the nesting birds.

3 My Life as a Saint

I still have the nest, now empty,
woven of my hair, of the hollow grass,
and silken tassels at the ends of seeds.
From the window where I prayed,
I saw the house wrens gather
dark filaments from air
in the shuttles of their beaks.
Then the cup was made fast
to the body of the tree,
bound with the silver excrescence of the spider,
and the eggs, four in number,
ale gold and trembling,
curved in a thimble of down.

The hinged beak sprang open, tongue erect,
screaming to be fed
before the rest of the hatchling emerged.
I did not eat. I smashed bread to crumbs upon the sill
for the parents were weary as God is weary.
We have the least mercy on the one
who created us,
who introduced us to this hunger.

The smallest mouth starved and the mother
swept it out like rubbish with her wing.
I found it that dawn, after lauds,

already melting into the heat of the flagstone,
a transparent teaspoon of flesh,
the tiny beak shut, the eyes still sealed
within a membrane of the clearest blue.

I buried the chick in a box of leaves.
The rest grew fat and clamorous.
I put my hands through the thorns one night and felt the bowl,
the small brown begging bowl,
waiting to be filled.

By morning, the strands of the nest disappear
into each other, shaping
an emptiness within me that I make lovely
as the immature birds make the air
by defining the tunnels and the spirals
of the new sustenance. And then,
no longer hindered by the violence of their need,
they take to other trees, fling themselves
deep into the world.

4 Agnes

When you entered the church at Basia
holding the scepter of the almond's
white branch, and when you struck
the bedrock floor, how was I to know
the prayer would be answered?
I heard the drum of hooves long in the distance,
and I held my forehead to the stone of the altar.
I asked for nothing. It is almost
impossible to ask for nothing.
I have spent my whole life trying.

I know you felt it, when his love spilled.
That ponderous light.
From then on you endured
happiness, the barge you pulled
as I pull mine. This
is called density of purpose.
As you learned, you must shed everything else
in order to bear it.

That is why, toward the end of your life
when at last there was nothing I could not relinquish,
I allowed you to spring forward without me.
Sister, I unchained myself. For I was always
the heaviest passenger,
the stone wagon of example,

the freight you dragged all the way to heaven,
and how were you to release yourself
from me, then, poor mad horse,
except by reaching the gate?

Mary Magdalene

I wash your ankles
with my tears. Unhem
my sweep of hair
and burnish the arch of your foot.
Still your voice cracks
above me.

I cut off my hair and toss it across your pillow.
A dark towel
like the one after sex.
I'm walking out,
my face a dustpan,
my body stiff as a new broom.

I will drive boys
to smash empty bottles on their brows.
I will pull them right out of their skins.
It is the old way that girls
get even with their fathers—
by wrecking their bodies on other men.

Christ's Twin

He was formed of chicken blood and lightning.
He was what fell out when the jug tipped.
He was waiting at the bottom
of the cliff when the swine plunged over.
He tore out their lungs with a sound like ripping silk.
He hacked the pink carcasses apart, so that the ribs spread
like a terrible butterfly, and there was darkness.
It was he who turned the handle and let the dogs
rush from the basements. He shoved the crust
of a volcano into his roaring mouth.
He showed one empty hand. The other gripped
a crowbar, a monkey wrench, a crop
which was the tail of the ass that bore them to Egypt,
one in each saddlebag, sucking twists
of honeyed goatskin, arguing
already over a woman's breasts.
He understood the prayers that rose
in every language, for he had split the human tongue.
He was not the Devil nor among the Fallen—
it was just that he was clumsy, and curious,
and liked to play with knives. He was the dove
hypnotized by boredom and betrayed by light.
He was the pearl in the mouth, the tangible
emptiness that saints seek at the center of their prayers.

He leaped into a shadow when the massive stone
rolled across the entrance, sealing him with his brother
in the dark as in the beginning.
Only this time he emerged first, bearing the self-
    inflicted wound, both brass halos
tacked to the back of his skull.
He raised two crooked fingers; the extra die
tumbled from his lips when he preached
but no one noticed. They were too busy
clawing at the hem of his robe and planning
how to sell him to the world.

Orozco's Christ

Who rips his own flesh down the seams and steps
forth flourishing the ax,
who chops down his own cross,
who straddles it,
who stares like a cat,
whose cheeks are the gouged blue of science,
whose torso springs out of wrung cloth
blazing ocher, blazing rust, whose blood
cools to black marble in his fist,
who makes his father kneel,
who makes his father say,
"You want her? Take her."
Who rolls the stone from the entrance over his mother,
who pulls her veil out from under it,
who ties the stained cloth around his hips
and starts out,
walking toward Jerusalem
where they are gathering in his name.

The Savior

When the rain began to fall, he rolled back
into the clouds and slept again.
Still it persisted, beating at every surface,
until it entered his body
as the sound of prolonged
human weeping.

So he was broken.
His first tears dissolved
the mask of white stone.
As they traveled through the bones of his arms,
his strength became a mortal strength,
subject to love.

On earth, when he heard the first rain
tap through the olive leaves,
he opened his eyes and stared at his mother.
As his father, who had made the sacrifice,
stood motionless in heaven,
his son cried out to him:

I *want no shelter, I deny*
the whole configuration.

I *hate the weight of earth.*
I *hate the sound of water.*
Ash to ash, you say, but I *know different.*
I *will not stop burning.*

The Buffalo Prayer

Our Lady of the Buffalo Bones, pray for us.
Our Lady of the bales of skins and rotting hulks
from which our tongues alone were taken,
pray for us, Our Lady of the Poisoned Meat
and of the wolves who ate
and whose tongues swelled until they burst.
Our Lady of the Eagles Dropping from the Sky,
Our Lady of the Sick Fox and of the Lurching Hawk
and of the hunters at the edge of Yellowstone Park waiting
to rain thunder on the last of us.
Pray for us, Our Lady of Polaris.
Our Lady of the Sleek Skidoo.
Our Lady of Destruction Everywhere
Our bones were ground into fertilizer
for the worn-out eastern earth.
Our bones were burned to charcoal
to process sugar and to make glue
for the shoe soles of your nuns and priests.
Our Lady of the Testicle Tobacco Pouch
Our Lady of the Box Cars of Skulls,
pray for us whose bones have nourished
the ordered cornfields that have replaced
the random grass
which fed and nurtured and gave us life.

Rez Litany

Let us now pray to those beatified
within the Holy Colonial church
beginning with Saint Assimilus,
patron of residential and of government
boarding schools, whose skin was dark
but who miraculously bled white milk
for all to drink.
To cure the gut aches that resulted
as ninety percent of Native children are
lactose intolerant, let us now pray to the
patron saint of the Indian Health Service,
who is also guardian of slot machines,
Our Lady of Luck, she who carries
in one hand mistaken blood tests and botched
surgeries and in the other hand the heart
of a courageous doctor squeezed dry.
Let us pray for the sacred hearts of all good doctors
and nurses, whose tasks are manifold and made more difficult
by the twin saints of commodity food,
Saint Bloatinus and Saint Cholestrus,
who were martyred at the stake of body fat
and who preside now in heaven
at the gates of the Grand Casino Buffet.
Saint Macaronia and Saint Diabeta, hear our prayer.

It is terrible to be diminished toe by toe.
Good Saint Pyromane,
Enemy of the BIA,
Deliver us from those who seek to bury us
in files and triplicate documents and directives.
Saint Quantum, Martyr of Blood
and Holy Protector of the Tribal Rolls,
assist us in the final shredding which shall proceed
on the Day of Judgment so we may all rain down
in a blizzard of bum pull tabs
and unchosen lottery tickets, which represent
the souls of the faithfully departed
in your name.
Your name written in the original fire
we mistook so long ago for trader's rum.
Pray for us, all you saints of white port
four roses old granddad and night train.
Good Saint Bingeous who fell asleep upside down on the cross
and rose on the third day without even knowing he had died.
Saint Odium of the hundred-proof blood
and Saint Tremens of the great pagan spiders
dripping from the light fixtures.
You powerful triumvirate, intercede for us
drunks stalled in the bars,
float our asses off the cracked stools
and over to the tribal college,
where the true saints are ready to sacrifice their brain cells
for our brain cells, in that holy exchange which is called learning.

Saint Microcephalia, patron of huffers and dusters,
you of the cooked brain and mean capacity, you
of the simian palm line and poor impulse control,
you of the Lysol-soaked bread, you sleeping with the dogs
underneath the house, hear our prayers
which we utter backwards and sideways
as nothing makes sense
least of all your Abstinence Campaign
from which Oh Lord Deliver Us.
Saints Primapara, Gravida, and Humpenenabackseat,
you patrons of unsafe teenage sex
and fourteen-year-old mothers,
pray for us now and at the hour of our birth,
amen.

Original Fire

The Fence

Then one day the gray rags vanish
and the sweet wind rattles her sash.
Her secrets bloom hot. I'm wild for everything.
My body is a golden armor around my unborn child's body,
and I'll die happy, here on the ground.
I bend to the mixture of dirt, chopped hay,
grindings of coffee from our dark winter breakfasts.
I spoon the rich substance around the acid-loving shrubs.
I tear down last year's drunken vines,
pull the black rug off the bed of asparagus
and lie there, knowing by June I'll push the baby out
as easily as seed wings fold back from the cotyledon.
I see the first leaf already, the veined tongue
rigid between the thighs of the runner beans.
I know how the shoot will complicate itself
as roots fill the trench.
Here is the link fence, the stem doubling toward it,
and something I've never witnessed.
One moment the young plant trembles on its stalk.
The next, it has already gripped the wire.
Now it will continue to climb, dragging rude blossoms
to the other side
until in summer fruit like green scimitars,

the frieze of vines, and then the small body
spread before me in need
drinking light from the shifting wall of my body,
and the fingers, tiny stems wavering to mine,
flexing for the ascent.

Ninth Month

This is the last month, the petrified forest
and the lake which has long since turned to grass.
The sun roars over, casting its light and absence
in identical seams. One day. Another.
The child sleeps on in its capsized boat.

The hull is weathered silver and our sleep is green and dark.
Dreams of the rower, hands curled in the shape of oars,
listening for the cries of the alabaster birds.
All is silent, the animals hurled into quartz.
Our bed is the wrecked blue island of time and love.

Black steeples, black shavings of magnetized iron,
through which the moon parades her wastes,
drawing the fruit from the female body,
pulling water like blankets up other shores.

Then slowly the sky is colored in, the snow
falls evenly into the blackness of cisterns.
The steel wings fan open that will part us from each other
and the waves break and fall according to their discipline.

Breath that moves on the waters.
Small boat, small rower.

Birth

When they were wild
When they were not yet human
When they could have been anything,
I was on the other side ready with milk to lure them,
And their father, too, each name a net in his hands.

New Mother

1

I am here to praise this body
on loan from the gods
by which we know the god in us
and see the god made earth,

pulled out blue and stunned into the lights.

2

Sometimes in the frenzy of first events
there comes to me a strange
declamatory awareness
as though my consciousness has stirred
from the heap of broken toys
and new toys
that is my baby's existence.
When I look into her eyes I see below
the surface of things
into the water of the other surface
through the layers of that surface
to the original fire.

3

When you wake sometimes, crying
in the pure desolation of the newly realized,
I dream you are drifting off
in your little boat.
I crawl to you like swimming and hold you in my arms
and then I wonder if it was cruel, yes, cruel,
to force you with such violence through my body.
To bring you here.
That is why, when I find you,
I lay my hands upon you
in so tender a way
that you do not feel me quite at first.
I draw you back and you are calmed.
That is why I touch you with a lightness
I can repeat nowhere else.
That is why these anxious pictures
of you, larger every month, and why I call
your name continually,
throwing it out like an anchor.

Sorrows of the Frog Woman

"Her fear was for her child. Searching all around, she saw the footprints of an enormous frog and with them, the tracks of the little dog, as if he had been dragged along on his paws. She knew then that it was the Frog Woman who had stolen her baby and knew by the tracks that the little dog had tried to hold back the cradle board with his teeth."

—from "Wampum Hair," a story
told by Nawaquay-geezhik
(Charles Kawbawgam)

1 *Transformation*

My husband was a prince who kissed me
until my eyes bulged and my skin
melted to a green film on my bones.
My mouth split my face
and I croaked, *take me, oh take me.*
So I was, deeper
into my startling new body.

As I sank back onto the wet springs
of my haunches, as I powerfully gathered
my tongue unfolded in a blur,

a sticky lasso,
and plucked a fly from his lapel—
my last wifely act.

2 Control

At first, I hated this body,
my lung-thin skin, my temptress spots.
I wanted red silk and you gave me this!
Advantages—my bones are bendable straws
through which I drink sun,
golden yolk, food of inner life, heat, tremendous wish.
And there is night and the many voices
seething delirium
universal mirrors that are my eyes
implacable gold

What you change cannot love you.
I told him that. He kissed me anyway.

3 Origin

I was hungry, so the author of all things
gave me the flies of sorrow to eat.
Gave me the underslung heroic couplets
of a man's breast to drink from.
Gave me the perfect nothing
of my own original soul
to dive and dive in never touching bottom.

Sometimes I have the memory of what it was like
to be truly lovely
to dance by candlelight and tear the filmy cotton lace
off my nipples and draw you in.
Sometimes I have the memory of what it was like
to be another kind of food.

4 King Black Snake

My god, my predator,
to get away from you I change shapes.
I become the laughter at my core.

Time

My breasts are soft.
My hair is dull.
I am growing into the body
of the old woman who will bear me
toward my death,
my death which will do me no harm.
Every day the calico cat returns from the fields
with a mouse in her jaws.
After every bite of the tender lawn, the ground squirrel
jerks and flinches,
but no hawk drops out of the sky.
The fat creature continues to eat, nervously
stuffing itself with pleasure.

I watch him as I drink from a bottle of grassy wine.

Why do I long
to be devoured and to forget
in life rather than in death?
What is the difference?

Spring Evening on Blind Mountain

I won't drink wine tonight
I want to hear what is going on
not in my own head
but all around me.
I sit for hours
outside our house on Blind Mountain.
Below this scrap of yard
across the ragged old pasture,
two horses move
pulling grass into their mouths, tearing up
wildflowers by the roots.
They graze shoulder to shoulder.
Every night they lean together in sleep.
Up here, there is no one
for me to fail.
You are gone.
Our children are sleeping.
I don't even have to write this down.

Blue

I have moved beyond my life
into the blueness of the tiny flower
called Sky Pilot.
The sheer stain of the petals
fills the sky in my heart.

Over the field,
two bluebirds pause
on shivering wings.
They could as well have been a less glorious
color, and the flowers too.

Why were we given this unearthly radiance, this blueness,
if not to seek it out, to love it with all our hearts?

Thistles

for Persia

Under ledge, under tar, under fill
under curved blue stone of doorsteps,
under the aggregate of lakebed rock,
under loss and under hard words,
under steamrollers
under your heart,
it doesn't matter. They can live forever.
The seeds of thistles
push from nowhere, forming a rose of spikes
that spreads all summer until it
stands in a glory of
needles, blossoms, blazing
purple clubs and fists.

Best Friends in the First Grade

I'm brave.
I'm kind.
These are our powers.
Boys are coming!
How about we lead them into a trap and run?
We're both the bravest twins.
Identicals.
Only you like blue.
And I like orange.
Remember you have to act like
me and I have to act like you?
Don't kill the spider.
I forgot the crocodile hole!
We both can't die.
Our special rope tells us what to do.
I got you. I won't let you fall.
I'll shoot the jump rope over to the other side.
The king is chasing.
The rainstorm has heard our plan. Oh,
they are following us. We will have no choice
but to marry now. You will be a daughter.
I will be the rainstorm's wife.
But watch out.
The king has poisonous teeth.

Little Blue Eyeglasses

for Aza

Little blue eyeglasses,
I give you the honored task
of assisting my youngest daughter
in her work, which is to see not only
general shapes but specific details
and minute variations in the color and texture
of objects ranging from immense
(Ocean. Sky.) To very tiny.
(Invertebrate hidden at edge of carpet)
Little blue eyeglasses,
I charge you with the solemn responsibility
of depth perception. Guide her steps
through dim corridors
and allow her to charge down
the staircase into my arms
without injury. Above all,
little blue eyeglasses,
train her eyes upon the truth
and let her eyes rest in the truth
and help her see within the truth the strength
to bear the truth.

Grief

Sometimes you have to take your own hand
as though you were a lost child
and bring yourself stumbling
home over twisted ice.

Whiteness drifts over your house.
A page of warm light
falls steady from the open door.

Here is your bed, folded open.
Lie down, lie down, let the blue snow cover you.

Wood Mountain

for Abel

The sky glows yellow over the tin hump
of Mount Anaeus, and below on the valley floor
the fog cracks and lifts.
Beyond it the throat of the river flares.
The river shakes its body
of terminal mirrors.

I saw you walk down the mountain yesterday.
You were wearing your stained blue jacket,
your cheap, green boots.
You disappeared into a tree
the way you always did, in grief.
I went looking for you.
In the orchard floored with delicate grass,
I lay down with the deer.
A sweet, smoky dust rose
from the dead silver of firs.

When I stand in the circle of their calm black arms
I talk to you. I tell you everything.
And you do not weep.

You accept
how it was
night came down.
Ice formed on your eyelids.
How the singing began, that was not music
but the cold heat of stars.

Wind runs itself beneath the dust like a hand
lifting a scarf.
Mother, you say, and I hold you.
I tell you I was wrong, I am sorry.
So we listen to the coyotes.
And their weeping is not of this earth
where it is called sorrow, but of another earth
where it is known as joy,
and I am able
to walk into the tree of forgiveness with you
and disappear there
and know myself.

Advice to Myself

Leave the dishes.
Let the celery rot in the bottom drawer of the refrigerator
and an earthen scum harden on the kitchen floor.
Leave the black crumbs in the bottom of the toaster.
Throw the cracked bowl out and don't patch the cup.
Don't patch anything. Don't mend. Buy safety pins.
Don't even sew on a button.
Let the wind have its way, then the earth
that invades as dust and then the dead
foaming up in gray rolls underneath the couch.
Talk to them. Tell them they are welcome.
Don't keep all the pieces of the puzzles
or the doll's tiny shoes in pairs, don't worry
who uses whose toothbrush or if anything
matches, at all.
Except one word to another. Or a thought.
Pursue the authentic—decide first
what is authentic,
then go after it with all your heart.
Your heart, that place
you don't even think of cleaning out.
That closet stuffed with savage mementos.
Don't sort the paper clips from screws from saved baby teeth
or worry if we're all eating cereal for dinner

again. Don't answer the telephone, ever,
or weep over anything at all that breaks.
Pink molds will grow within those sealed cartons
in the refrigerator. Accept new forms of life
and talk to the dead
who drift in through the screened windows, who collect
patiently on the tops of food jars and books.
Recycle the mail, don't read it, don't read anything
except what destroys
the insulation between yourself and your experience
or what pulls down or what strikes at or what shatters
this ruse you call necessity.

Morning Fire

My baby, eating rainbows of sun
focused through a prism in my bedroom window,
puts her mouth to the transparent fire,
and licks up the candy colors
that tremble on the white sheets.
The stain spreads across her face.
She has only one tooth,
a grain of white rice
that keeps flashing.
She keeps eating as the day begins
until the rainbows are all inside of her.
And then she smiles
and such a light pours over me.
It is not that white blaze
that strikes the earth all around you
when you learn of the death
of one you love. Or the next light
that strips away your skin.
Not the radiance
that unwraps you to the bone.
Soft and original fire,
allow me to curl around you in the white sheets
and keep feeding you the light

from my own body
until we drift into the deep
of our being.
Air, fire, golden earth.

Asiniig

The Ojibwe word for stone, asin, is animate. Stones are alive. They are addressed as grandmothers and grandfathers. The universe began with a conversation between stones.

1

A thousand generations of you live and die
in the space of a single one of our thoughts.
A complete thought is a mountain.
We don't have very many ideas.

When the original fire which formed us
subsided,
we thought of you.
We allowed you to occur.
We are still deciding whether that was
wise.

2 Children

We have never denied you anything
you truly wanted
no matter how foolish
no matter how destructive
but you never seem to learn.

That which you cry for,
this wish to be like us,
we have tried to give it to you
in small doses, like a medicine, every day
so you will not be frightened.
Still, when death comes
you weep,
you do not recognize it
as the immortality you crave.

3 The Sweat Lodge

We love it when you sing to us,
and speak to us,
and lift us from the heart of the fire
with the deer's antlers, and place us
in the center of the lodge.
Then we are at our most beautiful,
Powerful red blossoms,
we are breathing.
We can reach through your bones
to where you hurt.
You call us grandfather, grandmother.
You scatter bits of cedar, sage, wikenh, tobacco
and bear root over us,
and then the water
which cracks us to the core.

When we break ourselves open—
that is when the healing starts.
When you break yourselves open—
that is how the healing continues.

4 Love

If only you could be more like us
when it comes to the affections.
Have you ever seen a stone
throw itself?
On the other hand
whose idea do you think it is
to fly through the air?
Mystery is not a passive condition.
To see a thing so perfectly what it is—
doesn't it make you
want to hold it,
to marvel, to touch
its answered question?

5 Gratitude

You have no call to treat us this way.
We allow you to put us to every use.
Yet, when have you ever
stopped in the street to lay your forehead
against the cool, black granite facade
of some building, and ask the stone
to bless you?
We are not impartial.
We acknowledge some forms
of consideration.
We open for those
who adhere to our one rule
endure.

6 Infinite Thought

Listen, there is no consciousness
before birth or
after death
except the one you share
with us.
So you had best learn
how to speak to us now
without the use of signs.
Remember, there will be no hands,
except remembered hands.
No lips, no face,
except remembered face.
No legs and in fact no
appendages, except
the remembered ones,
which always hurt
as consciousness hurts.
Now do you understand what it is?
Your consciousness
is the itch, the ghost of consciousness,
remembered
from how it felt
to be one of us.

ALSO BY LOUISE ERDRICH

FUTURE HOME OF THE LIVING GOD A Novel
Available in Hardcover, E-Book, Large Print, and Digital Audio

LAROSE A Novel
Available in Paperback, E-Book, Audio, and Large Print

THE ROUND HOUSE A Novel
Winner of the National Book Award for Fiction
Available in Paperback, E-Book, Audio, and Large Print

SHADOW TAG A Novel • Available in Paperback and Large Print

THE PLAGUE OF DOVES A Novel
Available in Paperback, E-Book, and Large Print

THE PAINTED DRUM A Novel • Available in Paperback, E-Book, and Large Print

FOUR SOULS A Novel • Available in Paperback and E-Book

THE MASTER BUTCHERS SINGING CLUB A Novel
Available in Paperback and E-Book

**THE LAST REPORT ON THE MIRACLES AT
LITTLE NO HORSE** A Novel • Available in Paperback and E-Book

ANTELOPE WOMAN A Novel • Available in Paperback and E-Book

TALES OF BURNING LOVE A Novel • Available in Paperback

THE BINGO PALACE A Novel • Available in Paperback

THE CROWN OF COLUMBUS
A Novel (co-written with Michael Dorris) • Available in Paperback

TRACKS A Novel • Available in Paperback

THE BEET QUEEN A Novel • Available in Paperback

LOVE MEDICINE A Novel • Available in Paperback

THE RED CONVERTIBLE Selected and New Stories, 1978-2008
Available in Paperback and Large Print

ORIGINAL FIRE Selected and New Poems
Available in Paperback and E-Book

THE BLUE JAY'S DANCE A Birth Year • Available in Paperback

BOOKS AND ISLANDS IN OJIBWE COUNTRY
Available in Paperback and E-Book